WELCOME TO
PASSPORT TO READING

A beginning reader's ticket to a brand-new world!

Every book in this program is designed to build read-along and read-alone skills, level by level, through engaging and enriching stories. As the reader turns each page, he or she will become more confident with new vocabulary, sight words, and comprehension.

These PASSPORT TO READING levels will help you choose the perfect book for every reader.

READING TOGETHER
Read short words in simple sentence structures together to begin a reader's journey.

READING OUT LOUD
Encourage developing readers to sound out words in more complex stories with simple vocabulary.

READING INDEPENDENTLY
Newly independent readers gain confidence reading more complex sentences with higher word counts.

READY TO READ MORE
Readers prepare for chapter books with fewer illustrations and longer paragraphs.

This book features sight words from the educator-[illegible]ted Dolch Sight Words List. This encourages the re[illegible]ze commonly used vocabulary words, i[illegible]d and fluency.

For more information, please visit pass[illegible]

Enjoy the jou[illegible]

Little, Brown and Company

Hachette Book Group
1290 Avenue of the Americas, New York, NY 10104
Visit us at lb-kids.com
bobthebuilder.com

Little, Brown and Company is a division of Hachette Book Group, Inc.
The Little, Brown name and logo are trademarks of Hachette Book Group, Inc.

The publisher is not responsible for websites (or their content) that are not owned by the publisher.

First Edition: July 2016

Library of Congress Control Number: 2016936595

ISBN 978-0-316-35682-4

10 9 8 7 6 5 4 3 2 1

CW

Printed in the United States of America

Passport to Reading titles are leveled by independent reviewers applying the standards developed by Irene Fountas and Gay Su Pinnell in *Matching Books to Readers: Using Leveled Books in Guided Reading*, Heinemann, 1999.

Lofty and the Giraffe

Adapted by Emily Sollinger
Based on the episode "Lofty Lets Loose"
by Laura Beaumont & Paul Larson

LITTLE, BROWN AND COMPANY
New York Boston

Attention, Bob the Builder fans!
Look for these words
when you read this book.
Can you spot them all?

giraffe

fence

rocks

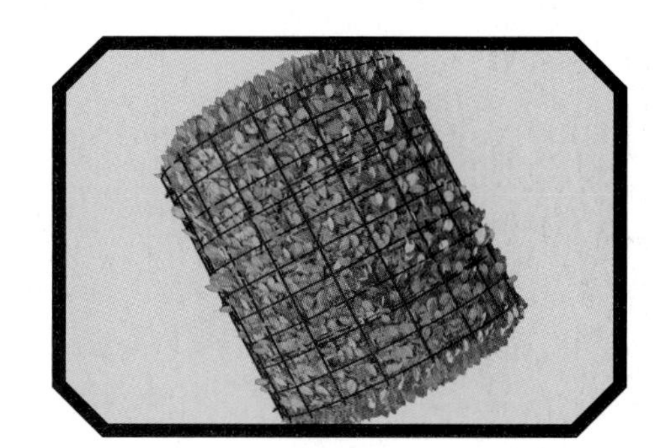

leaves

Bob was excited.

A giraffe was coming to Fixham Zoo.

“Hello, team!” said Bob.
“We will build a home for the giraffe.”
“Hooray!” said the team.

“I love giraffes!” Lofty said.
“They have long necks, just like me!”

"Can we build it?" Bob asked.
"Yes, we can!" said the team.

“I hope the giraffe will like his new home,” worried Jenny the zookeeper. “I am sure he will love it!” said Bob.

Lofty lifted the supplies over the fence.
Scoop drilled holes.

Wendy and Bob put the posts in place.

Dizzy poured the cement.

Lofty lifted the last few rocks.

Lofty was excited to meet the giraffe.

"I know all about giraffes!" he said.

Soon the giraffe arrived.

“Welcome to Fixham Zoo,” said Jenny.

Lofty could not see the giraffe.

The fence was too high.

Lofty tried to peek through the fence.

Crash!
The fence fell down.

The noise scared the giraffe.

The giraffe ran away.

"I am sorry!" Lofty said.
"I broke the fence and scared away the giraffe."

“Do not worry, Lofty!” said Bob.
“We will fix it!”

Wendy, Leo, and Scoop worked on the fence.

The rest of the team looked for the giraffe.
They could not find him.

Lofty had an idea.
"The giraffe will come out if he sees food!"
Lofty picked up a bale of leaves.

Bob climbed aboard Lofty.

They drove slowly through the zoo.

"Lofty, look!" said Bob.
The giraffe walked toward them.

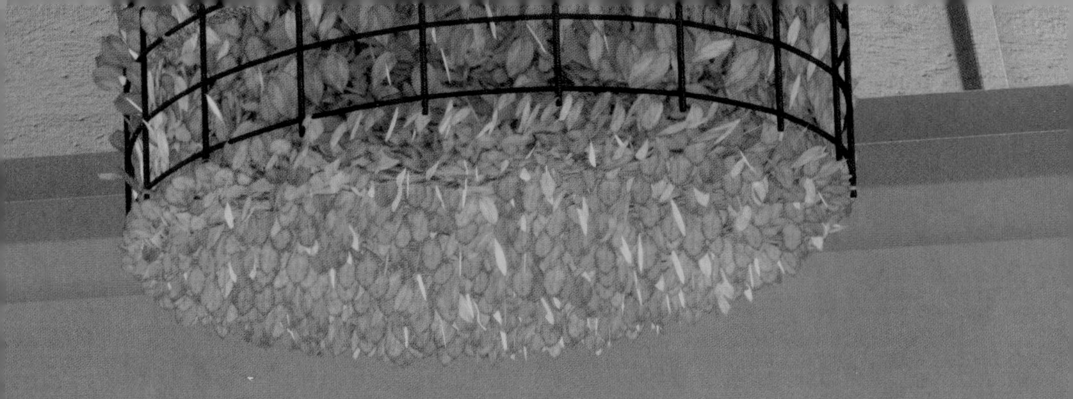

The giraffe nibbled the leaves.
Lofty led the giraffe back to
his home.

Wendy and Leo opened the gate.
Lofty put down the bale of leaves.

The giraffe followed.

Wendy and Leo shut the gate.

The giraffe crunched and munched the leaves.

Scoop, Dizzy, and Lofty watched.

“Thank you, Bob, and your team, for your great work,” said Jenny.

“I will name him Lofty the giraffe,”
Jenny added.
“After Lofty the crane, who helped find him!”

“Hello, Lofty!” said Lofty the crane to his new friend, Lofty the giraffe.